This book belongs to:

For Lars and Oliver
Brigita

For Aurelia and Raihan
Jennie

First published in the United Kingdom in 2019 by Lantana Publishing Ltd., London.
www.lantanapublishing.com

American edition published in 2019 by Lantana Publishing Ltd., UK.
info@lantanapublishing.com

A CIP catalogue record for this book is available from the British Library.

Distributed in the United States and Canada by Lerner Publishing Group, Inc.
241 First Avenue North, Minneapolis, MN 55401 U.S.A.
For reading levels and more information, look for this title at www.lernerbooks.com
Cataloging-in-Publication Data Available.

Printed and bound in Europe.
Original art created with mixed media and natural textures, completed digitally.

ISBN: 978-1-911373-87-2
eBook ISBN: 978-1-911373-90-2

The Pirate Tree

LANTANA PUBLISHING

The gnarled tree on the hill sometimes turns into a pirate ship. A rope serves as an anchor, a sheet as a sail, and Sam is its fearless captain.

Today, the tree watches as another sailor approaches.

“Can I play?” Agu asks, standing on the ship’s leeward side.

Sam hoists the sheet up over a branch and glares.

“I don’t know you. You’re not from my street.”

Agu's face falls. He watches her struggle with a thick rope. No one wants to play with him because he's a newcomer.

“Beware, here come pirates!” Sam yells. “ARRR!”

When Sam doesn’t as much as look his way, Agu’s shoulders slump. Auntie told him to be patient, but he’s been patient for days.

"We go sailing the warm south seas," Sam sings,
"stealing cargo off mighty ships,
robbing diamonds in Nigeria,
gold from—"

Agu snorts. “There are no diamonds in Nigeria.”

Sam pauses. The sheet collapses as she lets go of the twine. “How do you know?”

"I used to live in Nigeria."

Sam's eyes widen. Then she frowns. "What else do you know?"

"I sailed on a ship. I can tell you about it," Agu says, his voice rising.

Sam shuffles her feet,
scratches her head
and pulls on her ear.
“Come on, then.”

They set sail again.

The breeze is generous and the ocean is wide before them.

They land on a deserted island and find fresh coconuts and precious seashells.

Agu shows Sam how to reef the mainsail when the wind gets fierce.

They spar with mean pirates from a rival ship and win.

They are about to round Cape Horn when Dad calls from the yard. “Sam, dinner time!”

“The cook is calling from the galley,” Sam says. “Let’s go and see what he’s caught.”

Agu coils the thick rope Sam uses for an anchor.

“What’s your name, then?” Sam asks, bunching the sheet under her arm.

“I’m Agu.”

They set off down the slope, treading through waves of grass.

“A cool name for a pirate,” Sam says.

“It means tiger.”

Sam grins at her
new crew member.
"You'll sail with me
again, won't you?"

They are too far away for the tree to hear Agu's answer. Its boughs sigh in the zephyr, waiting for the day it will turn into a pirate ship once again and sail the distant seas with the two new friends.